A MEMBER of the FAMILY

MADELINE SUNSHINE

SCHOLASTIC BOOK SERVICES
New York Toronto London Auckland Sydney Tokyo

Illustrated by Catherine Huerta

This book is from Sprint Starter Library B.
Other titles in this library are:
The Haunted House
Kitchen Caper
The Mad Doctor
Pirate Kite

Copyright © 1978 by Scholastic Magazines, Inc. All rights reserved. Published by Scholastic Book Services, a division of Scholastic Magazines, Inc.

12 11 10 9 8 7 6 5 4 3 2 1   9   8 9/7 0 1 2 3/8

Printed in the U.S.A.   09

A MEMBER of the FAMILY

CATHERINE HUERTA

CHAPTER 1

Mitchell raced out of the school building. Soon he was outside. He looked around. Cathy, Neal, and Mark were already waiting for him.

Mitchell could not believe it. He had made three new friends. He'd only been living in this neighborhood for one week. Maybe things were really going to be different here.

"Well, let's get going," said Mark. The four kids began walking down the street.

"Whose house are we going to today?" asked Cathy.

Mitchell was silent. He hoped they wouldn't ask him again. He had run out of excuses.

"We can't go to mine," said Neal. "It's being painted."

"Don't look at me," laughed Mark. "We were there yesterday. My mother could not take two days in a row!"

"How about your house, Cathy?" Mark asked. "We could play ping-pong there."

"No way!" said Cathy. "I told you this morning. My parents are having company tonight."

"I guess we will have to go to Mitchell's house," Mark said.

"Right," said Cathy. "We've never been there. It will be fun."

"We can't," said Mitchell. "I...I forgot my keys," he said. "And no one is home."

"Again!" exclaimed Mark. "That's exactly what you said yesterday."

"Are you calling me a liar?" Mitchell shouted. "I said you can't come to my house! Not now and not ever!"

The other kids looked at Mitchell in surprise.

"Oh, no," thought Mitchell. "I should never have said that. They probably all hate me now." Mitchell began to run down the street.

"Where are you going?" Cathy shouted. "Come back!"

Mitchell didn't turn around. He just kept on running.

CHAPTER 2

Neal, Cathy, and Mark looked down the street. They watched as Mitchell disappeared from sight. Then they began walking.

"Boy, was that strange!" exclaimed Cathy. "Why do you think he ran away? What did we do to make him so angry?"

"I don't know," said Neal. "And I'm beginning not to care! He is starting to bug me. He says he likes us. But sometimes he sure does not act that way!"

"Right," agreed Mark. "He hangs out with us. He comes to all our houses. But every time we mention his, he's got an excuse."

"You mean a lie!" said Neal.

"Don't say that," said Cathy. "Who knows? He could have a real reason for not letting us visit him. Maybe he's very poor or something. He might not want us to find out."

"You could be right," said Mark. "Or maybe it's his mother and father. Maybe they won't let him have friends over."

"Hold on!" said Neal. "I'll bet it's something else. His parents may be spies. Or maybe his house is haunted. Maybe it's a hiding place for robbers!"

"Listen," said Mark. "I have an idea. Why don't we go find out? Mitchell only lives a few blocks away."

"I don't know," said Neal. "It may be dangerous."

Mark and Cathy looked at one another. They wondered if Neal really was scared. They were starting to feel a little nervous. Finally, they made up their minds. Each of them took a deep breath. Then they set out for Mitchell's house.

CHAPTER 3

Mitchell didn't stop running until he reached his house. He rang the bell again and again. At last, his mother opened the door. He pushed past her and dashed inside.

"Hurry!" he said. "Close the door. They may have followed me."

"What!" exclaimed his mother. "Who may have followed you? Mitchell, are you in trouble?"

"No, no," Mitchell said. "It's Neal, Mark, and

Cathy. They wanted to come over today. I didn't know what to do. So I ran away from them."

"But why?" asked his mother. "You know your friends are welcome to visit. I've always told you that."

"You know why!" shouted Mitchell. "It's her — Gloria! Why can't you understand?" he cried. "I could have had a chance here. It's a new neighborhood. I was making new friends. Then they wanted to come over here. Don't you see? I could not let them. They don't know about Gloria yet. And they are not going to find out!"

"Mitchell," said his mother. "You can't keep Gloria a secret forever. She's a member of our family!"

"I don't care!" screamed Mitchell. "She spoils everything for me! Even when she's not there!"

Mitchell's mother shook her head sadly. "It hurts me when you talk about her this way," she said. "We are going to have to discuss this later." His mother put on her coat. She walked over to the door.

"Where are you going?" Mitchell asked.

"Shopping," answered his mother. "I'll be back in a little while. And please don't forget to...."

"I know!" Mitchell said. "Don't forget to take care of Gloria!"

CHAPTER
4

Mark, Neal, and Cathy were walking down one street after another.

"Boy," grumbled Cathy. "How come it's taking so long to get to Mitchell's house? I hope you know where you're going, Mark!"

"Of course I do," he replied. "I already told you. I saw the address on Mitchell's notebook. We're almost there now."

At last Mark stopped. "That's it," he said pointing. "The big gray house across the street."

"Well," said Cathy. "It does not look scary from here. Come on, let's go check it out."

They hurried across the street. They went up to the door. Then they rang the bell. No one answered. They waited for a minute and then rang again.

"Well, I guess that's that," said Neal. "Now we can get out of here. No one is home."

"Wait!" cried Cathy. "Did you hear that?"

"Hear what?" asked Mark. "What were we supposed to hear?"

"A voice," answered Cathy. "I'm sure I heard a voice."

"That's impossible," said Mark. "Where could it be coming from? We are the only ones here."

"I'm telling you, I heard something," Cathy insisted.

"Ghosts!" said Neal. "That's what it is. I knew it all along. This house is haunted."

"Cut it out," Mark said angrily. "Quit trying to scare us. There is no such thing as...."

Mark's sentence ended right there. Cathy grabbed his arm. He stopped speaking. Then they all heard it. It was a voice all right. It was a strange, high voice.

"Listen!" cried Cathy. "It's coming from around there." She pointed toward the back of the house. Then she began to run. "Follow me," she called out. "Hurry!"

15

CHAPTER 5

Cathy ran across the front lawn. "So this is what Mitchell's house looks like," she said to herself. She turned back. Mark was right behind her. Neal was also behind her.

"Let's follow this walkway," Cathy said. "It leads to the back of the house."

"We had better be careful," said Mark. "We don't know what's back there."

When they got to the other side of the house, they stopped short. They saw a girl who looked their age. She was sitting on a swing.

Someone was standing behind her, pushing her back and forth. That someone was Mitchell! As the swing moved, the girl began to say the alphabet.

"A, B, C, D, E, F, G," she said. When she finished, she turned to Mitchell.

"Gloria do good?" she asked.

"Perfect!" replied Mitchell with a big smile.

Just then, he heard a noise. Mitchell spun around and saw Mark, Cathy, and Neal. His smile quickly disappeared.

"What are you doing here?" yelled Mitchell. "I told you not to come here!"

Cathy, Neal, and Mark were silent. They didn't know what to say.

"Stop staring!" Mitchell screamed. "What's the matter! Haven't you ever seen a dummy before? That's right!" he shouted. "My sister is a dummy! She is retarded. Go on, say it! Everyone else does! Mitchell's sister is a dummy!"

"No!" cried Gloria, jumping off the swing. "I am not a dummy! No dummy!" She began to cry. Before Mitchell could say more, she ran out of the yard.

"Go on, Gloria! Run!" screamed Mitchell. Then suddenly he stopped yelling. "What am I saying?" he cried. "Gloria! Please, come back!"

CHAPTER
6

Mitchell ran after his sister.

"Gloria, come back!" he shouted.

Gloria would not turn around. "Bad Mitchell!" she called. "Bad, bad!"

"Please stop, Gloria," cried Mitchell. "If you come back, we can play!"

Gloria still didn't stop. She put her hands over her ears. "No!" she cried. "No, no, no!" She ran all the way across the lawn. She didn't stop until she reached the street.

Mitchell could not believe what was happening. Gloria had never done this before. He kept chasing her. His mind was racing. His eyes would not focus. He could barely see. And that's how it happened! He tripped over a rock and fell down hard.

"Help me! Please, help me!" he called.

Cathy, Neal, and Mark hurried toward him.

Mitchell looked up and down the street. There was no sign of Gloria anywhere. It was almost as though she had vanished. He closed his eyes. He really felt like crying. When he opened them again, Cathy, Neal, and Mark were there. Cathy and Neal leaned down toward Mitchell. They pulled him to his feet.

"Are you all right?" asked Mark.

"I'm not sure," said Mitchell. "My leg hurts. But it's not me I'm worried about. It's Gloria! Please, you've got to help me. She's never been on the street alone before. She could get hurt out there. She does not understand about crossing streets. And she talks to people — strangers! Please, you've got to help me find her. You've just got to!"

23

CHAPTER 7

Neal, Cathy, and Mark looked all around them. Gloria was still nowhere in sight. They weren't sure how to get started. Finally, Neal had an idea.

"We'll have to split up," he said. "It's the only way to cover both sides of the street." He pointed toward a row of trees. "Mark, you and Cathy go up that way. Mitchell and I will head in the other direction. Let's go!"

Cathy and Mark ran toward the trees.

"Come on, Mitchell," said Neal. "Put your arm around my shoulder. I will help you."

"No," said Mitchell. "I'll only slow you down. You go ahead."

"OK," Neal said. "Don't worry, Mitchell. We'll find her. I promise." With that, he took off.

Mitchell was alone now. He began to think about Gloria. But just then, something caught his eye. He saw a car door open all by itself. He leaned forward to get a better look. Now he could see a girl climbing out of it. It was her!

"Gloria! Gloria!" he yelled. "Wait for me! I'll be right there!"

Gloria stopped. She knew someone was calling her. But she could not tell where the voice came from.

"Mark! Cathy!" Mitchell yelled. "It's Gloria! She's over there — near the red car!"

Cathy and Mark came running. They called out to Gloria as they ran.

Gloria looked around. She saw two figures coming toward her. Suddenly she became afraid. She started to run away from them. She jumped off the sidewalk. She ran into the street without looking.

"Gloria, watch out!" Mitchell shouted. "There's a car coming!"

CHAPTER 8

A car was headed in Gloria's direction.
Cathy, Mark, and Neal raced toward her.
Cathy was in the lead. Mark waved his hands
over his head. He was trying to signal the
driver. He was trying to make him stop. Cathy
reached Gloria. She grabbed her arm. She
pulled her over onto the sidewalk. The car
whizzed by. It was going fast. It would never
have been able to stop in time.

"Hi," said Gloria. "You want to come to my house? We can play. I got toys!"

Cathy was silent. She was still too shaken to talk.

"Don't you want to be my friend?" asked Gloria.

"Of course I do," Cathy finally answered.

"Good," said Gloria. "Then let's play. Where's Mitchell? He loves to play."

"I know," said Cathy. "I know your brother. I'm his friend."

"I'm his friend too," said Mark, joining them.

Mitchell hurried over to his sister. "I'm sorry, Gloria," he said. "I didn't mean to call you a dummy. I love you."

Gloria smiled. "We can play now, OK?" she asked.

"OK," said Mitchell.

Then he turned to Cathy, Neal, and Mark. "Thanks for helping me," he said. "But the show is over now. So, why don't you just go home!"

He took Gloria's hand. Then they turned and began to walk quickly away.

CHAPTER 9

Mitchell and his sister kept walking. Mark, Cathy, and Neal stared after them.

"He's really something," Mark finally said. "I mean, we saved his sister's life. He could have been a little nicer."

"Come on," said Neal. "He was pretty upset. Besides, this whole thing was our fault."

"Our fault!" exclaimed Mark. "He's the one who called Gloria names! That's why she ran away!"

"Yes, but we got him angry," replied Neal. "He told us not to come here. We should never have gone sneaking around his house."

"Maybe not," said Cathy. "But he was wrong too. And I'm going to tell him!"

She dashed off after Mitchell and Gloria. Neal and Mark followed close behind.

"You know what, Mitchell!" yelled Cathy. "You called Gloria a dummy before. But she's not the dummy! You are!"

"You don't understand!" cried Mitchell. "Where I used to live, everyone made fun of Gloria. And they made fun of me too. I never had any friends! Not ever!"

"Well, maybe that was your fault," said Neal.

"Right," said Mark. "Maybe you never tried. Sure, some kids are mean. But most aren't. Take us for instance. We wanted to be your friends. But you never gave us a chance!"

"We like you," said Cathy. "And now we like Gloria too. Why can't we all be friends?"

Before Mitchell could answer, his mother appeared.

"Where have you been?" she cried. "I was really worried. Is everything all right?"

"Everything is fine," said Mitchell. He
realized that Neal, Mark, and Cathy were right.
"Mother, I want you to meet Neal, Cathy, and
Mark — they're my friends."

"And mine too?" asked Gloria.

"And yours too," said Mitchell, hugging her
happily. "And yours too!"